The Fermata

By

E. T. A. Hoffmann

British Library Cataloguing-in-Publication Data
A catalogue record for this book is available from the
British Library

E. T. A. Hoffman

Ernst Theodor Wilhelm Hoffmann was born in Königsberg, East Prussia in 1776. His family were all jurists, and during his youth he was initially encouraged to pursue a career in law. However, in his late teens Hoffman became increasingly interested in literature and philosophy, and spent much of his time reading German classicists and attending lectures by, amongst others, Immanuel Kant.

In was in his twenties, upon moving with his uncle to Berlin, that Hoffman first began to promote himself as a composer, writing an operetta called Die Maske and entering a number of playwriting competitions. Hoffman struggled to establish himself anywhere for a while, flitting between a number of cities and dodging the attentions of Napoleon's occupying troops. In 1808, while living in Bamberg, he began his job as a theatre manager and a music critic, and Hoffman's break came a year later, with the publication of Ritter Gluck. The story centred on a man who meets, or thinks he has met, a long-dead composer, and played into the 'doppelgänger' theme – at that time very popular in literature. It was shortly after this that Hoffman began to use the pseudonym E. T. A. Hoffmann, declaring the 'A' to stand for 'Amadeus', as a tribute to the great composer, Mozart.

Over the next decade, while moving between Dresden, Leipzig and Berlin, Hoffman produced a great range of both literary and musical works. Probably Hoffman's most well-known story, produced in 1816, is 'The Nutcracker and the Mouse King', due to the fact that – some seventy-six years later - it inspired Tchaikovsky's ballet The Nutcracker.

In the same vein, his story 'The Sandman' provided both the inspiration for Léo Delibes's ballet Coppélia, and the basis for a highly influential essay by Sigmund Freud, called 'The Uncanny'. (Indeed, Freud referred to Hoffman as the "unrivalled master of the uncanny in literature.")

Alcohol abuse and syphilis eventually took a great toll on Hoffman though, and – having spent the last year of his life paralysed – he died in Berlin in 1822, aged just 46. His legacy is a powerful one, however: He is seen as a pioneer of both Romanticism and fantasy literature, and his novella, Mademoiselle de Scudéri: A Tale from the Times of Louis XIV is often cited as the first ever detective story.

The Fermata

Hummel's1 amusing, vivacious picture, "Company in an Italian Inn," became known by the Art Exhibition at Berlin in the autumn of 1814, where it appeared, to the delight of all who saw and studied it An arbour almost hidden in foliage — a table covered with wine-flasks and fruits — two Italian ladies sitting at it opposite each other, one singing, the other playing a guitar; between them, more in the background, stands an abbot, acting as music-director. With his baton raised, he is awaiting the moment when the Signora shall end, in a long trill, the cadence which, with her eyes directed heavenwards, she is just in the midst of; then down will come his hand, whilst the guitarist gaily dashes off the dominant chord. The abbot is filled with admiration — with exquisite delight — and at the same time his attention is painfully on the stretch. He wouldn't miss the proper downward beat for the world. He hardly dare breathe. He would like to stop the mouth and wings of every buzzing bee and midge. So much the more therefore is he annoyed at the bustling host who must needs come and bring the wine just at this supreme, delicious moment. An outlook upon an avenue, patterned by brilliant strips of light! There a horseman has pulled up, and a glass of something refreshing to drink is being handed up to him on horseback.

Before this picture stood the two friends Edward and Theodore. "The more I look at this singer," said Edward, "in her gay attire, who, though rather oldish, is yet full of the true inspiration of her art, and the more I am delighted with the grave but genuine Roman profile and lovely form of the guitarist, and the more my estimable friend the abbot amuses me, the more does the whole picture seem to me instinct with free, strong, vital power. It is plainly a caricature in the higher sense of the term, but rich in grace and vivacity. I should just like to step into that arbour and open one of those dainty little flasks which are ogling me from the table. I tell you what, I fancy I can already smell something of the sweet fragrance of the noble wine. Come, it were a sin for this solicitation to be wasted on the cold senseless atmosphere that is about us here. Let us go and drain a flask of Italian wine in honour of this fine picture, of art, and of merry Italy, where life is exhilarating and given for pleasure."

Whilst Edward was running on thus in disconnected sentences, Theodore stood silent and deeply absorbed in reflection. "Ay, that we will, come along," he said, starting up as if awakening out of a dream; but nevertheless he had some difficulty in tearing himself away from the picture, and as he mechanically followed his friend, he had to stop at the door to cast another longing lingering look back upon the singer and guitarist and abbot. Edward's proposal easily admitted of being carried into execution. They crossed the street diagonally, and very soon a flask exactly like those in the picture stood before them in Sala Tarone's2 little blue room. "It seems to me," said Edward, as Theodore still continued very silent and thoughtful, even after several glasses had been drunk, "it seems to me that the picture has made a deeper impression upon you than upon me, and not such an agreeable impression either." "I assure you," replied Theodore, "that I lost nothing of the brightness and grace of that animated composition; yet it is very singular,— it is a faithful representation of a scene out of my own life, reproducing the portraits of the parties concerned in it in a manner startlingly lifelike. You will, however, agree with me that diverting memories also have the power of strangely moving the mind when they suddenly spring up in this extraordinary and unexpected way, as if awakened by the wave of a magician's wand. That's the case with me just now." "What! a scene out of your own life!" exclaimed Edward, quite astonished. "Do you mean to say the picture represents an episode in your own life? I saw at once that the two ladies and the priest were eminently successful portraits, but I never for a moment dreamed that you had ever come across them in the course of your life. Come now, tell me all about it, how it all came about; we are quite alone, nobody else will come at this time o' day." "Willingly," answered Theodore, "but unfortunately I must go a long way back — to my early youth in fact." "Never mind; fire away," rejoined Edward; "I don't know over much about your early days. If it lasts a good while, nothing worse will happen than that we shall have to empty a bottle more than we at first bargained for; and to that nobody will have any objection, neither we, nor Mr. Tarone."

"That, throwing everything else aside, I at length devoted

myself entirely to the noble art of music," began Theodore, "need excite nobody's astonishment, for whilst still a boy I would hardly do anything else but play, and spent hours and hours strumming on my uncle's old creaking, jarring piano. The little town was very badly provided for music; there was nobody who could give me instruction except an old opinionated organist; he, however, was merely a dry arithmetician, and plagued me to death with obscure, unmelodious toccatas and fugues. But I held on bravely, without letting myself be daunted. The old fellow was crabby, and often found a good deal of fault, but he had only to play a good piece in his own powerful style, and I was at once reconciled both with him and with his art. I was then often in a curious state of mind; many pieces particularly of old Sebastian Bach were almost like a fearful ghost-story, and I yielded myself up to that feeling of pleasurable awe to which we are so prone in the days of our fantastic youth. But I entered into a veritable Eden when, as sometimes happened in winter, the bandmaster of the town and his colleagues, supported by a few other moderate dilettante players, gave a concert, and I, owing to the strict time I always kept, was permitted to play the kettledrum in the symphony. It was not until later that I perceived how ridiculous and extravagant these concerts were. My teacher generally played two concertos on the piano by Wolff or Emanuel Bach,3 a member of the town band struggled with Stamitz,4 while the receiver of excise duties worked away hard at the flute, and took in such an immense supply of breath that he blew out both lights on his music-stand, and always had to have them relighted again. Singing wasn't thought about; my uncle, a great friend and patron of music, always disparaged the local talent in this line. He still dwelt with exuberant delight upon the days gone by, when the four choristers of the four churches of the town agreed together to give Lottchen am Hofe.5 Above all, he was wont to extol the toleration which united the singers in the production of this work of art, for not only the Catholic and the Evangelical but also the Reformed community was split into two bodies — those speaking German and those speaking French. The French chorister was not daunted by the Lottchen, but, as my uncle maintained, sang his part, spectacles on nose, in the finest falsetto that ever proceeded forth from a human breast. Now there was amongst us (I mean in the town) a spinster named Meibel, aged about fifty-five, who subsisted upon the scanty pension which she received as a retired court singer of the metropolis, and my uncle was rightly of opinion that Miss Meibel might still do something for her money in the concert hall. She assumed airs of importance, required a good deal of coaxing, but at last consented, so that we came to have bravurasin our concerts. She was a singular creature this Miss Meibel. I still retain a lively recollection of her lean little figure. Dressed in a many-coloured gown, she was wont to step forward with her roll of music in her hand, looking very grave and solemn, and to acknowledge the audience with a slight inclination of the upper part of her body. Her head-dress was a most remarkable head-dress. In front was fastened a nosegay of Italian flowers of porcelain, which kept up a strange trembling and tottering as she sang. At the end, after the audience had greeted her with no stinted measure of applause, she proudly handed the music-roll to my uncle, and permitted him to dip his thumb and finger into a little porcelain snuff-box, fashioned in the shape of a pug dog, out of which she took a pinch herself with evident relish. She had a horrible squeaky voice, indulged in all sorts of ludicrous flourishes and roulades, and so you may imagine what an effect all this, combined with her ridiculous manners and style of dress, could not fail to have upon me. My uncle overflowed with panegyrics; that I could not understand, and so turned the more readily to my organist, who, looking with contempt upon vocal efforts in general, delighted me down to the ground as in his hypochondriac malicious way he parodied the ludicrous old spinster.

"The more decidedly I came to share with my master his contempt for singing, the higher did he rate my musical genius. He took a great and zealous interest in instructing me in counterpoint, so that I soon came to write the most ingenious toccatas and fugues. I was once playing one of these ingenious specimens of my skill to my uncle on my birthday (I was nineteen years old), when the waiter of our first hotel stepped into the room to announce the visit of two foreign ladies who had just arrived in the town. Before my uncle could throw off his dressing-gown — it was of a large flower pattern — and don his coat and vest, his visitors were already in the room. You know what an electric effect every strange event has upon those who are brought up in the narrow seclusion of a small country town; this in particular, which crossed my path so unexpectedly, was preeminently fitted to work a complete revolution within me. Picture to yourself two tall, slender Italian ladies, dressed fantastically and in bright colours, quite up to the latest fashion, meeting my uncle with the freedom of professional artistes, and yet with considerable charms of manner, and addressing him in firm and sonorous voices. What the deuce of a strange tongue they speak! Only now and then does it sound at all like German. My uncle doesn't understand a word; embarrassed, mute as a maggot, he steps back and points to the sofa. They sit down, talk together — it sounds like music itself. At length they succeed in making my good uncle comprehend that they are singers on a tour; they would like to give a concert in the place, and have come to him, as he is the man to conduct such musical negotiations.

"Whilst they were talking together I picked up their Christian names, and I fancied that I could now more easily and more distinctly distinguish the one from the other, for their both making their appearance together had at first confused me. Lauretta, apparently the elder of the two, looked about her with sparkling eyes, and talked away at my embarrassed old uncle with gushing vivacity and with demonstrative gestures. She was not too tall, and of a voluptuous build, so that my eyes wandered amid many charms that hitherto had been strangers to them. Teresina, taller, more slender, with a long grave face, spoke but seldom, but what she did say was more intelligible. Now and then a peculiar smile flitted across her features; it almost seemed as if she were highly amused at my good uncle, who had withdrawn into his silken dressing-gown like a snail into its shell, and was vainly endeavouring to push out of sight a treacherous yellow string, with which he fastened his night-jacket together, and which would keep tumbling out of his bosom yards and yards long. At length they rose to depart; my uncle promised to arrange everything for the concert for the third day following; then the sisters gave him and me, whom he introduced to them as a young musician, a most polite invitation to take chocolate with them in the afternoon.

"We mounted the steps with a solemn air and awkward gait; we both felt very peculiar, as if we were going to meet some adventure to which we were not equal. In consequence of due previous preparation my uncle had a good many fine things to say about art, which nobody understood, neither he himself nor any of the rest of us. This done, and after I had thrice burned my tongue with the scalding hot chocolate, but with the stoical fortitude of a Scævola had smiled under the fiery infliction, Lauretta at length said that she would sing to us. Teresina took her guitar, tuned it, and struck a few full chords. It was the first time I had heard the instrument, and the characteristic mysterious sounds of the trembling strings made a deep and wonderful impression upon me. Lauretta began very softly and held on, the note rising to fortissimo , and then quickly broke into a crisp complicated run through an octave and a half. I can still remember the words of the beginning, 'Sento l'amica speme.' My heart was oppressed; I had never had an idea of anything of the kind. But as Lauretta continued to soar in bolder and higher flights, and as the musical notes poured upon me like sparkling rays, thicker and thicker, then was the music that had so long lain mute and lifeless within me enkindled, rising up in strong, grand flames. Ah! I had never heard what music was in my life before! Then the sisters sang one of those grand impressive duets of Abbot Steffani6 which confine themselves to notes of a low register. My soul was stirred at the sound of Teresina's alto, it was so sonorous, and as pure as silver bells. I couldn't for the life of me restrain my emotion; tears started to my eyes. My uncle coughed warningly, and cast angry glances upon me; it was all of no use, I was really quite beside myself. This seemed to please the sisters; they began to inquire into the nature and extent of my musical studies; I was ashamed of my performances in that line, and with the hardihood born of enthusiastic admiration, I bluntly declared that that day was the first time I had ever heard music. 'The dear good boy!' lisped Lauretta, so sweetly and bewitchingly.

"On reaching home again, I was seized with a sort of fury: I pounced upon all the toccatas and fugues that I had hammered out, as well as a beautiful copy of forty-five variations of a canonical theme that the organist had written and done me the honour of presenting to me,— all these I threw into the fire, and laughed with spiteful glee as the double counterpoint smoked and crackled. Then I sat down at the piano and tried first to imitate the tones of the guitar, then to play the sisters' melodies, and finished by attempting to sing them. At length about midnight my uncle emerged from his bedroom and greeted me with, 'My boy, you'd better just stop that screeching and troop off to bed;' and he put out both candles and went back to his own room. I had no other alternative but to obey. The mysterious power of song came to me in my dreams — at least I thought so — for I sang 'Sento l'amica speme' in excellent style.

"The next morning my uncle had hunted up everybody who could fiddle and blow for the rehearsal. He was proud to show what good musicians the town possessed; but everything seemed to go perversely wrong. Lauretta set to work at a fine scene; but very soon in the recitative the orchestra was all at sixes and sevens, not one of them had any idea of accompaniment Lauretta screamed — raved — wept with impatience and anger. The organist was presiding at the piano; she attacked him with the bitterest reproaches. He got up and in silent obduracy marched out of the hall. The bandmaster of the town, whom Lauretta had dubbed a 'German ass!' took his violin under his arm, and, banging his hat on his head with an air of defiance, likewise made for the door. The members of his company, sticking their bows under the strings of their violins, and unscrewing the mouthpieces of their brass instruments, followed him. There was nobody but the dilettanti left, and they gazed about them with disconsolate looks, whilst the receiver of excise duties exclaimed, with a tragic air, 'O heaven! how mortified I feel!' All my diffidence was gone,— I threw myself in the bandmaster's way, I begged, I prayed, in my distress I promised him six new minuets with double trios for the annual ball. I succeeded in appeasing him. He went back to his place, his companions followed suit, and soon the orchestra was reconstituted, except that the organist was wanting. He was slowly making his way across the market-place, no shouting or beckoning could make him turn back. Teresina had looked on at the whole scene with smothered laughter, while Lauretta was now as full of glee as before she had been of anger. She was unstinted in her praise of my efforts; she asked me if I played the piano, and ere I knew what I was about, I sat in the organist's place with the music before me. Never before had I accompanied a singer, still less directed an orchestra. Teresina sat down beside me at the piano and gave me every time; Lauretta encouraged me with repeated 'Bravos!' the orchestra proved manageable, and things continued to improve. Everything was worked out successfully at the second rehearsal; and the effect of the sisters' singing at the concert is not to be described.

"The sovereign's return to his capital was to be celebrated there with several festive demonstrations; the sisters were summoned to sing in the theatre and at concerts. Until the time that their presence was required they resolved to remain in our little town, and thus it came to pass that they gave us a few more concerts. The admiration of the public rose to a kind of madness. Old Miss Meibel, however, took with a deliberate air a pinch of snuff out of her porcelain pug and

mata*

gave her opinion that 'such impudent caterwauling was not singing; singing should be low and melodious.' My friend, the organist, never showed himself again, and, in truth, I did not miss him in the least I was the happiest fellow in the world. The whole day long I spent with the sisters, copying out the vocal scores of what they were to sing in the capital. Lauretta was my ideal; her vile caprices, her terribly passionate violence, the torments she inflicted upon me at the piano — all these I bore with patience. She alone had unsealed for me the springs of true music. I began to study Italian, and try my hand at a few canzonets. In what heavenly rapture was I plunged when Lauretta sang my compositions, or even praised them. Often it seemed to me as if it was not I who had thought out and set what she sang, but that the thought first shone forth in her singing of it. With Teresina I could not somehow get on familiar terms; she sang but seldom, and didn't seem to make much account of all that I was doing, and sometimes I even fancied that she was laughing at me behind my back. At length the time came for them to leave the town. And now I felt for the first time how dear Lauretta had become to me, and how impossible it would be for me to separate from her. Often, when she was in a tender, playful mood, she had caressed me, although always in a perfectly artless fashion; nevertheless, my blood was excited, and it was nothing but the strange coolness with which she was more usually wont to treat me that restrained me from giving reins to my ardour and clasping her in my arms in a delirium of passion. I possessed a tolerably good tenor voice, which, however, I had never practised, but now I began to cultivate it assiduously. I frequently sang with Lauretta one of those tender Italian duets of which there exists such an endless number. We were just singing one of these pieces, the hour of departure was close at hand —'Senza di te ben mio, vivere non poss' io' ('Without thee, my own, I cannot live!') Who could resist that? I threw myself at her feet — I was in despair. She raised me up —'But, my friend, need we then part?' I pricked up my ears with amazement. She proposed that I should accompany her and Teresina to the capital, for if I intended to devote myself wholly to music I must leave this wretched little town some time or other. Picture to yourself one struggling in the dark depths of boundless despair, who has given up all hopes of life, and who, in the moment in which he expects to receive the blow that is to crush him for ever, suddenly finds himself sitting in a glorious bright arbour of roses, where hundreds of unseen but loving voices whisper, 'You are still alive, dear,— still alive'— and you will know how I felt then. Along with them to the capital! that had seized upon my heart as an ineradicable resolution. But I won't tire you with the details of how I set to work to convince my uncle that I ought now by all means to go to the capital, which, moreover, was not very far away. He at length gave his consent, and announced his intention of going with me. Here was a tricksy stroke of fortune! I dare not give utterance to my purpose of travelling in company with the sisters. A violent cold, which my uncle caught, proved my saviour.

"I left the town by the stage-coach, but only went

as far as the first stopping-station, where I awaited my divinity. A well-lined purse enabled me to make all due and fitting preparations. I was seized with the romantic idea of accompanying the ladies in the character of a protecting paladin — on horseback; I secured a horse, which, though not particularly handsome, was, its owner assured me, quiet, and I rode back at the appointed time to meet the two fair singers. I soon saw the little carriage, which had two seats, coming towards me. Lauretta and Teresina sat on the principal seat, whilst on the other, with her back to the driver, sat their maid, the fat little Gianna, a brown-cheeked Neapolitan. Besides this living freight, the carriage was packed full of boxes, satchels, and baskets of all sizes and shapes, such as invariably accompany ladies when they travel. Two little pug-dogs which Gianna was nursing in her lap began to bark when I gaily saluted the company.

"All was going on very nicely; we were traversing the last stage of the journey, when my steed all at once conceived the idea that it was high time to be returning homewards. Being aware that stern measures were not always blessed with a remarkable degree of success in such cases, I felt advised to have recourse to milder means of persuasion; but the obstinate brute remained insensible to all my well-meant exhortations. I wanted to go forwards, he backwards, and all the advantage that my efforts gave me over him was that instead of taking to his heels for home, he continued to run round in circles. Teresina leaned forward out of the carriage and had a hearty laugh; Lauretta, holding her hands before her face, screamed out as if I were in imminent danger. This gave me the courage of despair, I drove the spurs into the brute's ribs, but that very same moment I was roughly hurled off and found myself sprawling on the ground. The horse stood perfectly still, and, stretching out his long neck, regarded me with what I took to be nothing else than derision. I was not able to rise to my feet; the driver had to come and help me; Lauretta had jumped out and was weeping and lamenting; Teresina did nothing but laugh without ceasing. I had sprained my foot, and couldn't possibly mount again. How was I to get on? My steed was fastened to the carriage, whilst I crept into it. Just picture us all — two rather robust females, a fat servant-girl, two pug-dogs, a dozen boxes, satchels, and baskets, and me as well, all packed into a little carriage. Picture Lauretta's complaints at the uncomfortableness of her seat, the howling of the pups, the chattering of the Neapolitan, Teresina's sulks, the unspeakable pain I felt in my foot, and you will have some idea of my enviable situation! Teresina averred that she could not endure it any longer. We stopped; in a trice she was out of the carriage, had untied my horse, and was up in the saddle, prancing and curvetting around us. I must indeed admit that she cut a fine figure. The dignity and elegance which marked her carriage and bearing were still more prominent on horseback. She asked for her guitar, then dropping the reins on her arm, she began to sing proud Spanish ballads with a full-toned accompaniment. Her light silk dress fluttered in the wind, its folds and creases giving rise to a sheeny play of light, whilst the white feathers of her hat quivered and shook, like the prattling spirits of the air which we heard in her voice. Altogether she made such a romantic figure that I could not keep my eyes off her, notwithstanding that Lauretta reproached her for making herself such a fantastic simpleton, and predicted that she would suffer for her audacity. But no accident happened; either the horse had lost all his stubbornness or he liked the fair singer better than the paladin; at any rate, Teresina did not creep back into the carriage again until we had almost reached the gates of the town.

"If you had seen me then at concerts and operas, if you had seen me revelling in all sorts of music, and as a diligent accompanist studying arias, duets, and I don't know what besides at the piano, you would have perceived, by the complete change in my behaviour, that I was filled with a new and wonderful spirit. I had cast off all my rustic shyness, and sat at the pianoforte with my score before me like an experienced professional, directing the performances of my prima donna. All my mind — all my thoughts — were sweet melodies. Utterly regardless of all the rules of counterpoint, I composed all sorts of canzonets and arias, which Lauretta sang, though only in her own room. Why would she never sing any of my pieces at a concert? I could not understand it. Teresina also arose before my imagination curvetting on her proud steed with the lute in her hands, like Art herself disguised in romance. Without thinking of it consciously, I wrote several songs of a high and serious nature. Lauretta, it is true, played with her notes like a capricious fairy queen.

There was nothing upon which she ventured in which she had not success. But never did a roulade cross Teresina's lips; nothing more than a simple interpolated note, at most a mordent; but her long-sustained tones gleamed like meteors through the darkness of night, awakening strange spirits, who came and gazed with earnest eyes into the depths of my heart. I know not how I remained ignorant of them so long!

"The sisters were granted a benefit concert; I sang with Lauretta a long scena from Anfossi.7 As usual I presided at the piano. We came to the last fermata. Lauretta exerted all her skill and art; she warbled trill after trill like a nightingale, executed sustained notes, then long elaborate roulades — a whole solfeggio. In fact, I thought she was almost carrying the thing too far this time; I felt a soft breath on my cheek; Teresina stood behind me. At this moment Lauretta took a good start with the intention of swelling up to a 'harmonic shake,' and so passing back into a tempo. The devil entered into me; I jammed down the keys with both hands; the orchestra followed suit; and it was all over with Lauretta's trill, just at the supreme moment when she was to excite everybody's astonishment. Almost annihilating me with a look of fury, she crushed her roll of music together, tore it up, and hurled it at my head, so that the pieces flew all over me. Then she rushed like a madwoman through the orchestra into the adjoining room; as soon as we had concluded the piece, I followed her. She wept; she raved. 'Out of my sight, villain,' she screamed as soon as she saw me. 'You devil, you've completely ruined me — my fame, my honour — and oh!

my trill. Out of my sight, you devil's own!' She made a rush at me; I escaped through the door. Whilst some one else was performing, Teresina and the music-director at length succeeded in so far pacifying her rage, that she resolved to appear again; but I was not to be allowed to touch the piano. In the last duet that the sisters sang, Lauretta did contrive to introduce the swelling 'harmonic shake,' was rewarded with a storm of applause, and settled down into the best of humours.

"But I could not get over the vile treatment which I had received at her hands in the presence of so many people, and I was firmly resolved to set off home next morning for my native town. I was actually engaged in packing my things together when Teresina came into my room. Observing what I was about, she exclaimed, astonished, 'Are you going to leave us?' I gave her to understand that after the affront which had been put upon me by Lauretta I could not think of remaining any longer in her society. 'And so,' replied Teresina, 'you're going to let yourself be driven away by the extravagant conduct of a little fool, who is now heartily sorry for what she has done and said. Where else can you better live in your art than with us? Let me tell you, it only depends upon yourself and your own behaviour to keep her from such pranks as this. You are too compliant, too tender, too gentle. Besides, you rate her powers too highly. Her voice is indeed not bad, and it has a wide compass; but what else are all these fantastic warblings and flourishes, these preposterous runs, these never-ending shakes, but delusive artifices of style, which people admire in the same way that they admire the foolhardy agility of a rope-dancer? Do you imagine that such things can make any deep impression upon us and stir the heart? The 'harmonic shake' which you spoilt I cannot tolerate; I always feel anxious and pained when she attempts it. And then this scaling up into the region of the third line above the stave, what is it but a violent straining of the natural voice, which after all is the only thing that really moves the heart? I like the middle notes and the low notes. A sound that penetrates to the heart, a real quiet, easy transition from note to note, are what I love above all things. No useless ornamentation — a firm, clear, strong note — a definite expression, which carries away the mind and soul — that's real true singing, and that's how I sing. If you can't be reconciled to Lauretta again, then think of Teresina, who indeed likes you so much that you shall in your own way be her musical composer. Don't be cross — but all your elegant canzonets and arias can't be matched with this single ——,' she sang in her sonorous way a simple devotional sort of canzona which I had set a few days before. I had never dreamed that it could sound like that I felt the power of the music going through and through me; tears of joy and rapture stood in my eyes; I seized Teresina's hand, and pressing it to my lips a thousand times, swore I would never leave her.

"Lauretta looked upon my intimacy with her sister with envious but suppressed vexation, and she could not do without me, for, in spite of her skill, she was unable to study a new piece without help; she read badly, and was rather uncertain in her time. Teresina, on the contrary, sang everything at sight, and her ear for time was unparalleled. Never did Lauretta give such free rein to her caprice and violence as when her accompaniments were being practised. They were never right for her; she looked upon them as a necessary evil; the piano ought not to be heard at all, it should always be pianissimo; so there was nothing but giving way to her again and again, and altering the time just as the whim happened to come into her head at the moment But now I took a firm stand against her; I combated her impertinences; I taught her that an accompaniment devoid of energy was not conceivable, and that there was a marked difference between supporting and carrying along the song and letting it run to riot, without form and without time. Teresina faithfully lent me her assistance. I composed nothing but pieces for the Church, writing all the solos for a voice of low register. Teresina, too, tyrannised over me not a little, to which I submitted with a good grace, since she had more knowledge of, and (so at least I thought) more appreciation for, German seriousness than her sister.

"We were touring in South Germany. In a little town we met an Italian tenor who was making his way from Milan to Berlin. My fair companions went in ecstasies over their countryman; he stuck close to them, cultivating in particular Teresina's acquaintance, so that to my great vexation I soon came to play rather a secondary part. Once, just as I was about to enter the room with a roll of music under my arm, the voices of my companions and the tenor, engaged in an animated conversation, fell upon my ear. My name was mentioned; I pricked up my ears; I listened. I now understood Italian so well that not a word escaped me. Lauretta was describing the tragical occurrence of the concert when I cut short her trill by prematurely striking down the concluding notes of the bar. 'A German ass!' exclaimed the tenor. I felt as if I must rush in and hurl the flighty hero of the boards out of the window, but I restrained myself. She then went on to say that she had been minded to send me about my business at once, but, moved by my clamorous entreaties, she had so far had compassion upon me as to tolerate me some time longer, since I was studying singing under her. This, to my utter amazement, Teresina confirmed. 'Yes, he's a good child,' she added; 'he's in love with me now and sets everything for the alto. He is not without talent, but he must rub off that stiffness and awkwardness which is so characteristic of the Germans. I hope to make a good composer out of him; then he shall write me some good things — for there's very little written as yet for the alto voice — and afterwards I shall let him go his own way. He's very tiresome with his billing and cooing and love-sick sighing, and he worries me too much with his wearisome compositions, which have been but poor stuff up to the present.' 'I at least have now got rid of him,' interrupted Lauretta; 'and Teresina, how the fellow pestered me with his arias and duets you know very well.' And now she began to sing a duet of my composing, which formerly she had praised very highly. The other sister took up the second voice, and they parodied me both in voice and in execution in the most shameful manner. The tenor laughed till the walls rang again. My limbs froze; at once I formed an irrevocable resolve. I quietly slipped away from the door back into my own room, the windows of which looked upon a side street. Opposite was the post-office; the post-coach for Bamberg had just driven up to take in the mails and passengers. The latter were all standing ready waiting in the gateway, but I had still an hour to spare. Hastily packing up my things, I generously paid the whole of the bill at the hotel, and hurried across to the post-office. As I crossed the broad street I saw the fair sisters and the Italian still standing at the window, and looking out to catch the sound of the post-horn. I leaned back in the corner, and dwelt with a good deal of satisfaction upon the crushing effect of the bitter scathing letter that I had left behind for them in the hotel."

With evident gratification Theodore tossed off the rest of the fiery Aleatico8 that Edward had poured into his glass. The latter, opening a new flask and skilfully shaking off the drops of oil9 which swam at the top, remarked, "I should not have deemed Teresina capable of such falseness and artfulness. I cannot banish from my mind the recollection of what a charming figure she made as she sat on horseback singing Spanish ballads, whilst the horse pranced along in graceful curvets." "That was her culminating point," interrupted Theodore; "I still remember the strange impression which the scene made upon me. I forgot my pain; she seemed to me like a creature of a higher race. It is indeed very true that such moments are turning-points in one's life, and that in them many images arise which time does not avail to dim. Whenever I have succeeded with any fine romance, it has always been when Teresina's image has stepped forth from the treasure-house of my mind in clear bright colours at the moment of writing it."

"But," said Edward, "but let us not forget the artistic Lauretta; and, scattering all rancour to the winds, let us drink to the health of the two sisters." They did so. "Oh," exclaimed Theodore, "how the fragrant breezes of Italy arise out of this wine and fan my cheeks,— my blood rolls with quickened energy in my veins. Oh! why must I so soon leave that glorious land again!" "As yet," interrupted Edward, "as yet in all that you have told me I can see no connection with the beautiful picture, and so I believe that you still have something more to tell me about the sisters. Of course I perceive plainly that the ladies in the picture are none other than Lauretta and Teresina themselves." "You are right, they are," replied Theodore; "and my ejaculations and sighs, and my longings after the glorious land of Italy, will form a fitting introduction to what I still have to say. A short time ago, perhaps about two years since, just before leaving Rome, I made a little excursion on horseback. Before an inn stood a charming girl; the idea struck me how nice it would be to receive a cup of wine at the hands of the pretty child. I pulled up before the door, in a walk so thickly planted on each side with shrubs that the sunlight could only make its way through in patches. In the distance I heard sounds of singing and the tinkling of a guitar. I pricked up my ears and listened, for the two female voices affected me somehow in a singular fashion; strangely enough dim recollections began to stir within my mind, but they refused to take definite shape. I dismounted and slowly drew near to the vine-clad arbour whence the music seemed to proceed, eagerly catching up every sound in the meantime. The second voice had ceased to sing. The first sang a canzonet alone. As I came nearer and nearer that which had at first seemed familiar to me, and which had at first attracted my attention, gradually faded away. The singer was now in the midst of a florid, elaborate fermata. Up and down she warbled, up and down; at length she stopped, holding a note on for some time. But all at once a female voice began to let off a torrent of abuse, maledictions, curses, vituperations! A man protested; a second laughed. The other female voice took part in the altercation. The quarrel continued to wax louder and more violent, with true Italian fury. At length I stood immediately in front of the arbour; an abbot rushes out and almost runs over me; he turns his head to look at me; I recognise my good friend Signor Lodovico, my musical news-monger from Rome. 'What in the name of wonder'— I exclaim. 'Oh, sir! sir!' he screams, 'save me, protect me from this mad fury, from this crocodile, this tiger, this hyæna, this devil of a woman. Yes, I did, I did; I was beating time to Anfossi's canzonet, and brought down my baton too soon whilst she was in the midst of the fermata; I cut short her trill; but why did I meet her eyes, the devilish divinity! The deuce take all fermatas, I say!' In a most curious state of mind I hastened into the arbour along with the priest, and recognised at the first glance the sisters Lauretta and Teresina. The former was still shrieking and raging, and her sister still seriously remonstrating with her. Mine host, his bare arms crossed over his chest, was looking on laughing, whilst a girl was placing fresh flasks on the table. No sooner did the sisters catch sight of me than they threw themselves upon me exclaiming, 'Ah! Signor Teodoro!' and covered me with caresses. The quarrel was forgotten. 'Here you have a composer,' said Lauretta to the abbot, 'as charming as an Italian and as strong as a German.' Both sisters, continually interrupting each other, began to recount the happy days we had spent together, to speak of my musical abilities whilst still a youth, of our practisings together, of the excellence of my compositions; never did they like singing anything else but what I had set. Teresina at length informed me that a manager had engaged her as his first singer in tragic casts for the next carnival; but she would give him to understand that she would only sing on condition that the composition of at least one tragic opera was intrusted to me. The tragic was above all others my special department, and so on, and so on. Lauretta on her part maintained that it would be a pity if I did not follow my bent for the light and the graceful, in a word, for opera buffa. She had been engaged as first lady singer for this species of composition; and that nobody but I should write the piece in which she was to appear was simply a matter of course. You may fancy what my feelings were as I stood between the two. In a word, you perceive that the company which I had joined was the same as that which Hummel painted, and that just at the moment when the priest is on the point of cutting short Lauretta's fermata." "But did they not make any allusion," asked Edward, "to your departure from them, or to the scathing letter?" "Not with a single syllable," answered Theodore, "and you may be sure I didn't, for I had long before banished all animosity from my heart, and come to look back upon my adventure with the sisters as a merry prank. I did, however, so far revert to the subject that I related to the priest how that, several years before, exactly the same sort of mischance befell me in one of Anfossi's arias as had just befallen him. I painted the period of my connection with the sisters in tragi-comical colours, and, distributing many a keen side-blow, I let them feel the superiority, which the ripe experiences, both of life and of art, of the years that had elapsed in the interval had given me over them. 'And a good thing it was,' I concluded, 'that I did cut short that fermata, for it was evidently meant to last through eternity, and I am firmly of opinion that if I had left the singer alone, I should be sitting at the piano now.' 'But, signor,' replied the priest, 'what director is there who would dare to prescribe laws to the prima donna? Your offence was much more heinous than mine, you in the concert hall, and I here in the leafy arbour. Besides, I was only director in imagination; nobody need attach any importance to that, and if the sweet fiery glances of these heavenly eyes had not fascinated me, I should not have made an ass of myself.' The priest's last words proved tranquillising, for, although Lauretta's eyes had begun to flash with anger as the priest spoke, before he had finished she was quite appeased.

"We spent the evening together. Many changes take place in fourteen years, which was the interval that had passed since I had seen my fair friends. Lauretta, although looking somewhat older, was still not devoid of charms. Teresina had worn better, without losing her graceful form. Both were dressed in rather gay colours, and their manners were just the same as before, that is, fourteen years younger than the ladies themselves. At my request Teresina sang some of the serious songs that had once so deeply affected me, but I fancied that they sounded differently from what they did when I first heard them; and Lauretta's singing too, although her voice had not appreciably lost anything, either in power or in compass, seemed to me to be quite different from my recollection of it of former times The sisters' behaviour towards me, their feigned ecstasies, their rude admiration, which, however, took the shape of gracious patronage, had done much to put me in a bad humour, and now the obtrusiveness of this comparison between the images in my mind and the not over and above pleasing reality, tended to put me in a still worse. The droll priest, who in all the sweetest words you can imagine was playing the amorosoto both sisters at once, as well as frequent applications to the good wine, at length restored me to good humour, so that we spent a very pleasant evening in perfect concord and gaiety. The sisters were most pressing in their invitations to me to go home with them, that we might at once talk over the parts which I was to set for them and so concert measures accordingly. I left Rome without taking any further steps to find out their place of abode."

"And yet, after all," said Edward, "it is to them that you owe the awakening of your genius for music." "That I admit," replied Theodore, "I owed them that and a host of good melodies besides, and that is just the reason why I did not want to see them again. Every composer can recall certain impressions which time does not obliterate. The spirit of music spake, and his voice was the creative word which suddenly awakened the kindred spirit slumbering in the breast of the artist; then the latter rose like a sun which can nevermore set. Thus it is unquestionably true that all melodies which, stirred up in this way, proceed from the depths of the composer's being, seem to us to belong to the singer alone who fanned the first spark within us. We hear her voice and record only what she has sung. It is, however, the inheritance of us weak mortals that, clinging to the clods, we are only too fain to draw down what is above the earth into the miserable narrowness characteristic of things of the earth. Thus it comes to pass that the singer becomes our lover — or even our wife. The spell is broken, and the melody of her nature, which formerly revealed glorious things, is now prostituted to complaints about broken soup-plates or ink-stains in new linen. Happy is the composer who never again so long as he lives sets eyes upon the woman who by virtue of some mysterious power enkindled in him the flame of music. Even though the young artist's heart may be rent by pain and despair when the moment comes for parting from his lovely enchantress, nevertheless her form will continue to exist as a divinely beautiful strain which lives on and on in the pride of youth and beauty, engendering melodies in which time after time he perceives the lady of his love. But what is she else if not the Highest Ideal which, working its way from within outwards, is at length reflected in the external independent form?"

"A strange theory, but yet plausible," was Edward's comment, as the two friends, arm in arm, passed out from Sala Tarone's into the street.

Footnotes

1 Johann Erdmann Hummel, born 1769, died 1852, a German painter, studied in Italy, painted various kinds of pieces, and also wrote treatises on perspective and kindred subjects. The picture here referred to became perhaps almost as much celebrated from the fact of its having suggested this amusing sketch to Hoffmann as for its intrinsic merits as a work of art.

2 The keeper of a well-known tavern in Berlin, at about the time when this tale was written, 1817 to 1820.

3 The third son of the Sebastian Bach — theBach — just mentioned above. He was sometimes called "the Berlin Bach," or "the Hamburg Bach."

4 See note, p. 12 above.

5 This was one of a species of musical composition called Singspiele, a development of the simple song or Lied, by Johann Adam Hiller, (properly Hüller), born 1728, died 1804.

6 Agostino Steffani, an Italian by birth (1655), spent nearly all his life in Germany at the courts of Munich and Hanover. He wrote several operas, and was renowned for his duets, motets, &c.

7 Pasquale Anfossi, an Italian operatic composer of the eighteenth century. He was for a time the fashion of the day at Rome, but occupies now only a subordinate rank amongst musicians.

8 A red, aromatic, sweet Italian wine, made chiefly at

Florence.

9 The wine was presumably in flasks of the usual Italian kind, bottles encased in straw or reed, &c., with oil on the top of the wine instead of a cork in the neck of the bottle.

www.ingramcontent.com/pod-product-compliance
Lightning Source LLC
Chambersburg PA
CBHW030531260626
47157CB00005B/1986